Mingyuan Hu

Mnemosyne

Hermits United
London · Paris

Published in Great Britain by Hermits United Ltd. 2022
Copyright © Mingyuan Hu 2022
Printed in France

A catalogue record for this book is available from the British Library
ISBN 978-1-9998833-3-1

www.hermits-united.com

Mnemosyne

- -   Olivier   9

—   Constance   41

—   Olivier   59

- -

Olivier

- -

I have stayed as far away as I could. Presently, I sit on the plane, Paris before me, New York behind.

Locking up my apartment this afternoon, I knew I would be gone long.

Constance phoned this morning, telling me maman had died. It sounded like the last straw.

She'd been distraught since the passing of William. Now she needs me, me who has been absent.

For the first time in forty years, I fly to France,

having nothing whence to run away.

You can't negotiate with fate.

Papa asked me, when I was five or six, if I'd like a little brother or sister. Why would I share what I have? I remember thinking distinctly. No, papa, I want you all to myself. Papa's eyes embraced me warmly. I had my way.

Constance arrived when I was fifteen. I suspected that she was a surprise maman had wanted.

When maman's little girl turned three, I went to the Juilliard School, and never looked back.

Once a year I visited, in summer. Maman and Constance stayed in Paris or voyaged abroad. Papa and I went to the forests in Brittany, or to the mountains in the Pyrénées.

After papa died, I returned no more.

I think I have only ever loved papa.

- -

We buried maman. After the service, at the cimetière du Montparnasse, at first I had difficulty locating papa's grave.

A tomb now for two.

Constance is breaking down; or is already broken. I do not know. She trembled all day in my arms.

In New York, my apartment is so empty that when I play the piano, I hear echoes.

Now I hear her weep, in the middle of the night, at the other end of my parents' house.

I barely know her, my sister. Now I look after her, until she gets better.

It is my responsibility, I suppose.

- -

Maman would scoff at me sometimes; kindly, with humour. Papa never did.

He accepted unconditionally his eccentric son.

He took everything on his shoulders, papa. As a child, I saw him as a camel. Maman was an ostrich.

All my life, I was on papa's shoulders. When I was away, he missed me. Each year, he waited for me.

The two of us in the forests or in the mountains, walking for hours on end, conversing, musing, respiring in each other's ambiance: those were his favourite days of the year.

As they were mine.

He never questioned my decisions.

He never asked me to change.

- -

Maman never understood why I stayed in New York.

Perhaps they loved each other too much, my parents. Their love left little room for anyone else.

Perhaps.

How Constance grew up to be an accomplished painter, I hardly know. At papa's funeral years ago, I saw her with her husband William. They looked deeply in love.

I am the oddball in the family. By all appearances, I am loveless.

--

I accompanied Constance to visit her therapist. On the way back, we walked along the Seine.

She spoke of maman's last days. She spoke about William.

When she spoke of William, it was as though he was still alive.

Maman, to me, seemed long dead. She had dementia. In her final years, she remembered only papa.

It couldn't have been easy for Constance.

William fell, last autumn, when hiking. His remains were lost in the Highlands.

Constance has not returned to their London home since.

- -

My sister's fragility, intense in its purity, is alien to me.

In a valiant attempt, I said we should go to London to confront reality.

Certainly, I want to help her heal. But might it push her further into her affliction?

She looked at me, startled. One week later, we asked her therapist, who welcomed the idea.

Something strange weighs on my shoulders, keeping me focused.

Responsibility, I assume.

- -

The Heath is breathtakingly beautiful in April.

Twice a day, we take hour-long strolls. Amidst trees, squirrels, birds, silence, Constance is in her element.

I see papa in her.

Giving solace is not my forte. My means is simple: I do not leave her side.

As we try and put in order William's belongings, Constance wants to leave them in drawers for the time being. I understand.

It seems the most natural thing that William's study stays intact, its door closed.

It seems the most natural thing that I do not go near it, for fear of disturbing it.

In the grand salon, the walls are covered with William's books. They breathe melancholy without their master, and seem welcoming despite their melancholy. Five or six armchairs emit an invitation. One is expected to take a book from any part of the library, walk no more than three steps to the nearest chair, sit down, and sink in.

- -

Of all places, it is in William's substantial library, which I have taken to devouring every evening, that I encounter a Bildungsroman that papa mentioned when I was little.

Papa had read the novel as a young man, for grand-papa had read it as a young man – an epic already forgotten in grand-papa's youth: *Jean-Christophe* by Romain Rolland.

I read the ten volumes in a week. I realise that, all his life, papa protected me as his own Christophe, a musical genius in moral solitude.

Only papa was mistaken. I am not that moral genius.

The book, as I read it, is a spiritual portrait of papa. Like Rolland, he early stopped believing in God, while his belief system remained Christian through and through: earnest, humble, universal.

Papa lived to love his fellow men.

I wish I'd read this bible of a bygone soul when I, too, was a young man.

- -

How come William had Rolland in his library?
I asked Constance.

A lettré reads other lettrés, was her response.

The ease with which she takes certain things
for granted leaves an impression on me.

It has only lately dawned on me: my little
sister, like papa, accepts me as I am – aloof,
elusive.

Despite her grief, she is gratified when talking
about William. So we talk about William.
A philosopher and a linguist, he had erratic
tastes, and filled his books with notes.

In *Jean-Christophe* he scribbled 'This is Confucian' next to the following:

> ... le petit puritain de quinze ans entendit la voix de son Dieu: [...] On ne vit pas pour être heureux. On vit pour accomplir ma Loi. Souffre. Meurs. Mais sois ce que tu dois être : – un Homme.

An odd remark on William's part. I wish I could have conversed with him.

- -

William's books take me on a journey unforeseen.

Last night, picking out Leibniz's *Monadologie* from the shelves, I expected to revisit a youthful reading that had erstwhile left me bewildered.

William's notes left me dumbstruck.

To the title page was glued a printed sheet, where William had written under a strange diagram:

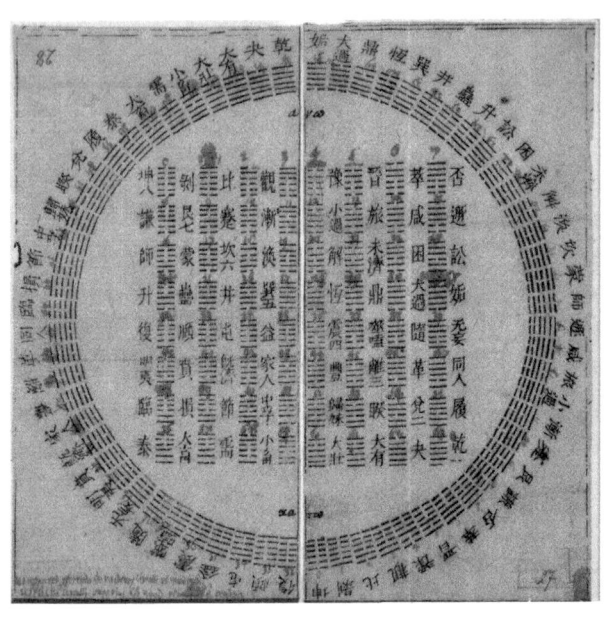

Imagine the monads as the lines.
Fancy the lines as monads.

Turning the page, I had intent to visualise, as per William's instruction, the 'monads' in the text as the 'lines' in the diagram.

The opening sections read altogether obscure.

In the margin I noticed William's handwriting:

> Replace 'substance' with 'line'. Replace 'compound' with 'hexagram'.

So I did. I began anew.

> *§1: La Monade, dont nous parlerons ici, n'est autre chose, qu'une substance simple, qui entre dans les composés; simple, c'est-à-dire sans parties.*

I read:

> The Monad is nothing other than a simple substance that is part of the compounds; simple meaning without parts.

... and re-read:

> The Monad is nothing other than a simple line that is part of the hexagrams; simple meaning without parts.

Quite, I observed.

> *§2: Et il faut qu'il y ait des substances simples, puisqu'il y a des composés; car le composé n'est autre chose, qu'un amas, ou aggregatum des simples.*

I read:

> There need be simple substances, for there are compounds; for the compound is nothing other than a pile or cluster of simples.

I re-read:

> There need be simple lines, for there are hexagrams; for the hexagram is nothing other than a pile or cluster of simples.

So it looked.

I continued:

> ... one wouldn't know how to transpose or conceive any internal movement in a monad [...] as one could in compounds, where there is change between the parts... (§7)

So, a line has no internal movement as hexagrams do. In the hexagrams, there is change between the lines...

Fair enough. Another look at the diagram confirmed the proposition.

> Each Monad has to be different from every other. (§9)

Each line has to be different from every other.

Poring over the diagram, I reckoned: on the

surface, there are but two types of line: broken and unbroken. For each line to be different from every other, that requires imagination…

But why not.

Looking again closely, I saw: each hexagram was different; and the difference, between every two neighbouring hexagrams, was one line and one line only.

Next to Leibniz's assertion – Each created being, as is the created monad, is subject to change, and this change within each is continuous (§10) – William had written:

> Each line in each hexagram is subject to change. The change within each is continuous.

The focus is now on change, I had a hunch.

The natural changes of Monads, expatiated Leibniz, come from an internal principle. (§11)

'In the world of the hexagrams,' wrote William, 'an internal principle of change governs.'

'But other than the principle of change,' wrote Leibniz, 'there need be a detail of that which changes, which is to say the specification and variety of simple substances.' (§12)

William noted:

> Specification and variety of the lines' changes define the 64 hexagrams.

Leibniz specified:

> This detail must encompass a multitude in the unity or in the simple. For natural change takes place by degrees; something changes and something stays... (§13)

Right. From one to the next, the hexagrams change by degrees; one line changes and others stay. The line changes from broken to unbroken, or from unbroken to broken; the changed line moves from one position to another, within the hexagram.

Each line, therefore, differs in its *actual or potential movement in relation to every other.*

- -

Deciphering thirteen sections of the *Monadologie* in this fashion quite exhausted me.

This morning, I rose early to resume the journey.

Leibniz is onto psychology, it occurs to me, when he names 'the passing state', that which represents a multitude in the unity, as 'perception' (§14).

We ourselves experience a multitude in the Simple Substance, he writes, when we find that 'the least thought we apperceive encompasses a variety in its object'. (§16)

As I replace 'Simple Substance' with 'Line' in my mind, and envision a multitude of experiences of the line in the diagram, William's comment comes to my rescue:

> A multitude in the Line and a variety in the thought's object recall the <u>act of divination</u>. Through chance operation, in the split second of a thought, one generates a hexagram out of 64; and is then taken to a specific <u>image</u> and presented with a variety of interpretations. Such interpretations are not set in stone, as some lines may be changing, others not. This, Bergson understood. Jung too.

I feel enlightened. I feel baffled. I give up.

Constance

—

Olivier looked puzzled this morning.

'I'm chewing on Leibniz's assertion that only monads with Memory are called souls,' he said.

'You are like William,' I replied.

He stared at me in incomprehension.

Twenty years ago, I said, William sat at breakfast wondering about the monads – or more precisely, about the *I Ching*.

'Do you mean the diagram?' He showed me William's book.

The diagram. We were awed by it, had fun with it, learned from it. And never understood it.

It understood us.

It's the human mind par excellence: at once the 'Soul with Memory' and the 'Kingdom of Moral Good' which Leibniz evoked, and which William unriddled.

William unriddled things, for his memory led him to see connections. Leibniz's coded language did not confound him, for he had read what Leibniz had read: the ancient Greeks, and the ancient Chinese.

Instinctively, he sensed the Chinese to be hovering behind the *Monadologie*. One cites the Sinophilism of Leibniz, he said, without knowing the exact chemical reaction ignited by this intellectual fascination.

To decrypt this chemical reaction, William and I packed our bags and headed to the Leibniz-Archiv.

That was in the early months of our courtship. I was smitten with William's mental energy and readiness for action, and followed him to many an archive and library, as he, just as willingly, accompanied me to many a museum, many a mountain, many a lake.

I still am. Smitten with William.

—

William's father was a diplomat. He retired early when William was fifteen.

'Diplomacy is about understanding where others are coming from, first and foremost,' he explained when he resigned. 'I'm afraid the function I'm serving today does little of that.'

This unfulfilled desire to understand others found expression in William's scholarship. William was the least prejudiced person I knew. He understood, for he wanted to. Because he wanted to, he found a way.

—

We sat in Hannover, William and I. For weeks we tried to digest the correspondence between Leibniz and Bouvet, a Jesuit missionary.

In 1700, from Pékin Bouvet sent Leibniz a diagram, seeing in the 'system of small lines' not just Leibniz's binary arithmetic, but a metaphysics, the profundity of which surpassed any known science.

William considered that Leibniz took his cue from Bouvet's letters in developing his monadic vision. The 'oneness', the 'very great unity' with which Bouvet grappled in the Chinese classics, became the 'unity' and the 'pre-established harmony' in Leibniz's world of monads.

What struck me was that, in the diagram, Bouvet determined sixty-four colours under eight principal classes; each class in turn contained eight different nuances.

Each of the sixty-four colours differs from its neighbours by only a degree. To Bouvet, this appeared as a universal nuance, to the extent that what could be said about colours could be said for all subjects operating with two principles – black and white, light and dark, wet and dry, hot and cold, zero and one, nothingness and oneness.

Everything, in this sense, differs only in terms of more or less. That 'more or less' is determined as much by itself as by its neighbours. All is relational – in colour as in perception. Therein lie the workings of change. Therein lies the working of the universe.

Bouvet marvelled at the visual philosophy conceived over 4,600 years ago.

So did we. Between the hexagrams and us, 5,000 years stand.

—

Reading Bouvet's letters to Leibniz, I remembered a painting I had seen when I was little.

Here, three-dimensional space is indicated by 'more or less' ink in each stroke and between neighbouring strokes. All is relational – in colour as in perception.

Isn't that why, to this day, Cézanne remains my favourite painter? As in the ink landscape, Cézanne's space is synonymous with colour relations.

In childhood, seeing the ink landscape in one of maman's books made me want to paint.

Aged nineteen, in art school, I heard from a professor: 'For the Chinese, ink has colours.' And I thought: quite right.

When I told William about the ink painting and about Cézanne, he reflected for a moment, and cited Bergson:

> Où il y a une fluidité de nuances fuyantes qui empiètent les unes sur les autres, elle aperçoit des couleurs tranchées, et pour ainsi dire solides, qui se juxtaposent comme les perles variées d'un collier : force lui est de supposer alors un fil, non moins solide, qui retiendrait les perles ensemble. Mais si ce substrat

> incolore est sans cesse coloré par ce qui le recouvre, il est pour nous, dans son indétermination, comme s'il n'existait pas. Or, nous ne percevons précisément que du coloré, c'est-à-dire des états psychologiques. [...] Mais quant à la vie psychologique, telle qu'elle se déroule sous les symboles qui la recouvrent, on s'aperçoit sans peine que le temps en est l'étoffe même.

What holds together coloured (perceivable) space and coloured (perceivable) psychological states, said William, is time, coloured by perception. Colourless, time is the actual material of life.

Returning from Hannover, William began to learn Chinese. I began to paint in ink.

—

Leibniz did not read Chinese. He believed the Chinese characters to have some interconnection. Bouvet came to read Chinese. He ratified Leibniz's impression.

Was Leibniz thinking of the Chinese characters when he wrote about the interconnectedness of monads and of composites? At breakfast, William continued to wonder.

The ink landscape which augured Cézanne and echoed Bergson continued to mesmerise me, decades after I first laid eyes on it. The painter, Gong Xian, died shortly after Bouvet arrived in Pékin from Brest. The landscape was one of Gong Xian's last.

As William read Leibniz and Bergson with different eyes, seeing before him the *I Ching* hexagrams, I painted with a different self-confidence, thinking about Cézanne and about Gong Xian.

Things are inter-connected for William.

They are inter-connected for me.

We are connected, he and I.

—

Olivier still looked puzzled.

Showing me one of William's hand-written notes in the *Monadologie*, he mumbled: 'Why *divination*? And what *image*?'

How do I begin?

I looked in the library. Wilhelm's take on the *I Ching* is by far the best, William once told me. As Olivier doesn't read German, I found for him Baynes' English translation of Wilhelm's German rendition.

'Read Jung's foreword,' I said, 'and we will enter the space.'

—

Olivier

—

Dialogue has consumed the day.

Constance's reminiscences. Her and William's connection to the hexagrams. My cluelessness. Their connectedness.

While I stay clueless, Constance is in the know. So I follow. I read Jung's foreword. I read Wilhelm's preface.

Unless I am mistaken, the *I Ching* has two components: the hexagrams and the text. In vulgar terms: image and word.

Unless I am mistaken, Leibniz and Bouvet looked at the hexagrams, overlooking the text. Wilhelm and Jung studied the text, which accompanied the hexagrams.

Leafing through the *I Ching*, I have the feeling that for its archaic makers, image and idea were one. And unless one treats them as one, one cannot grasp that which is whole.

Unless I am mistaken.

—

Not that I am at ease with all this.

I see the book has been of divinatory use for 5,000 years. Now I recall the anecdote, heard in my youth, that John Cage consulted an ancient book when he composed, asking questions and receiving answers through chance operation. This method, with its apparent irrationality, did not sit well with me.

In my youth I composed. My work – if I may thus call it, infrequently played as it has been – was of redoubtable precision, for want of a better description, more like Bach with a modern tinge than perhaps anything else.

But I was no Bach, evidently. In me there was never the mystic awe of a Christian; I pursued precision of only a mathematical kind.

Now with hindsight, I wonder if my precision was not, in fact, of only a mechanical kind, mathematics being awe-inspiring, for Bach as for Cage.

I wonder if this is not why, to hit the nail on the head, not even in comparison with Bach but simply with Cage, what I composed never had a veritable grandeur.

The grandeur of the heart.

—

I look at the *I Ching* in my hands.

So this was the book in question.

What trust Cage must have had to let go like this – but trust in what, I wonder.

Something more clairvoyant than his own intelligence?

But then, one must trust enough one's own intelligence to receive another's clairvoyance.

The clairvoyance of a book that speaks back.

—

Awaking from a night of agitated sleep, in the morning I tell Constance of my cerebration.

By way of response, she recalls that Bouvet wrote to Leibniz about the lost ancient music in China related to the hexagrams, a music in harmony with the celestial movements.

'Sounds Pythagorean to me,' I say. 'But if it were true, could anything be more mysterious?'

'Barely,' Constance concedes.

You are the musician in the family, she adds.

—

The musician in the family knows nothing.

Bach was a contemporary of Bouvet's – of that much I am aware. Did they know things that we've forgotten?

Can I unlearn what I've learned to remember that which I don't?

Days passed. This evening, looking at the sunset from the kitchen window, I asked Constance: 'Show me how to speak to the *I Ching*.'

She looked at me. She looked at me smilingly. It was her first smile since maman's death.

I translated her smile: I am proud of you, of your openness to the unknown.

I smiled back.

'William and I had been more resistant at the beginning,' said Constance, her eyes animated.

I followed her to William's study. She took out three medieval coins from one of the drawers.

'We always used these coins,' she said. 'Now you'll start by asking the book a question.'

—

Even more than what the book told Cage, I gathered, it was what Cage had asked the book that mattered.

I asked Constance: what was your first question, do you remember?

'I do, actually. I had the cheek to ask a humorous question. And I had a humorous answer.'

'And William's question?'

'A serious one.'

'Did he have a serious answer?'

'Dead serious.'

'I see.'

Our questions reveal us.

We sat down again at the kitchen table, when a thought overwhelmed me:

Why am I here?

—

Why am I here with my little sister, whom I had avoided ever since (or long before) she was born?

Why am I sipping tea in her kitchen, and not playing the piano in my New York apartment?

For what reason do I gaze at a diagram in William's book, wondering why I never composed anything of grandeur?

Just what is it that makes others love, trust, and bond – and me, loveless and clueless?

—

'Why am I here?'

'Hmm?' inquired Constance.

'Why am I here? – that is my question.'

'Ask it, loud at clear, to the book,' she said, 'and think about it while tossing three coins all at once, six times in a row.'

I did. After each tossing, Constance noted the heads or tails of each coin.

Then she looked in the book.

'Yang yin yin; yin yin yin: Return,' she said.

'What?'

'The 24th hexagram, *fu*, thunder within the earth: the image of the Turning Point. "Return" is the judgement. You have a six in the second place, meaning "Quiet Return". You have a six in the fifth place, meaning "Noblehearted Return".'

I did not know what to say.

She read out: 'After a time of decay comes the turning point. The powerful light that has been banished returns. There is movement, but it is not brought about by force. The upper trigram K'un is characterised by devotion; thus the movement is natural, arising spontaneously... Return is the stem of character... Return leads to self-knowledge.'

She looked up from the book: 'Maman always said you'd come back one day.'

'When … did she say that?'

'Always. Even when she remembered only papa, I saw it in her eyes when she looked at your photographs.'

I did not know what to say.

'Maman was right,' Constance smiled, again. 'And the book knows it too.'

—

I do not know what to say.

Did maman know that my return would be not only physical but metaphysical?

Need there be a 'why' in 'why I am here'?

I am here.

All in the nature of things. All in its own time.

—

Later, I found William's commentary written in the margins of Bergson's *Évolution créatrice*:

> If time is the actual material of life, if time is that which holds everything together, memory is that which holds time together, that which gives meaning to life.
>
> For lived moments are short, their psychic effects long. Our consciousness moves as occurrences move – like the small lines in the hexagrams move – from one state to the next, in the river of time.

—

I make rapprochements with William's mental space. I translate his commentary thus:

Life is graspable insomuch as a river is graspable.

It is intelligible insomuch as a world of 64 hexagrams is intelligible.

—

I go further: life resembles the world of hexagrams insomuch as change is its own cause; it is its own consequence.

The world of 64 hexagrams, that of black and white, zero and one, is one of infinite tones and possibilities. A divinatory reading, perchance, takes the pulse of moving consciousness and occurrence as they are singularly constellated in a given moment.

—

Somewhere William noted: for the ancient Greeks, divination was a limpid thought process. Constance tells: without qualms, Leibniz and Bouvet named the *I Ching* a monument of science.

Two centuries later, Wilhelm and Jung could no longer make like suggestions without making apologies, anticipating objection.

In some parts of the world, perceptions shifted more in those two centuries than in the preceding two millennia.

—

Summer came and went. In the symphony of autumnal wind, leaves began to fall, one by one.

I encountered William's annotation in Legge's translation of the *I Ching*:

> The moderns call science that which is deductible.
>
> The ancients called science that which is illuminating.

I would have liked to have known William better, I said to my sister.

—

Constance is painting again. I believe she is on the mend.

Last night I dreamt. I dreamt of musical notes as monades. Geometric sketches morphed into notations. Notations morphed into measuredly changing hexagrams. Each note, for a time, differed from its antecedent by one temporal or spatial extent. A diagram was in the making, sublime as a Gregorian chant.

I awoke, with an immense urge to compose. Not to be precise, but to be One with the cosmos.

Appendix

Rolland:

... the young puritan of fifteen heard the voice of his God: [...] One does not live to be happy. One lives to accomplish my Law. Suffer. Die. But be what you must be – a Man.

Bergson:

Where there is a flow of shifty nuances impinging upon one another, it perceives distinct and, so to speak, solid colours, placed side by side like varied beads of a necklace. It must perforce then imagine a string, no less solid, that holds the beads together. But if this colourless substrate is ceaselessly coloured by that which surrounds it, it is for us, in its indeterminateness, as if it did not exist. Yet, we perceive precisely only that which is coloured, that is to say psychological states. [...] But as regards the psychological life such as it unfolds under the symbols that cover it, we can easily see that time is its very material.

Further Reading

Henri Bergson, *L'évolution créatrice*. Paris: Felix Alcan, 1907.

James Legge (tr.), *The Yi King*, in *Sacred Books of the East*, vol. XVI. Oxford: Clarendon Press, 1882.

Gottfried Wilhelm Leibniz, *Monadologie*. Paris: Poussielgue frères, 1882.

Leibniz korrespondiert mit China: der Briefwechsel mit den Jesuitenmissionaren (1689-1714). Frankfurt am Main: V. Klostermann, 1990.

Romain Rolland, *Jean-Christophe*. Paris: Ollendorff, 1922-23.

Richard Wilhelm (tr.), *I Ging. Das Buch der Wandlungen*. Jena: Eugen Diederichs, 1924.

Richard Wilhelm (tr.), Cary Baynes (tr.), *I Ching: the Book of Changes*. New York: Pantheon Books, 1950.

This work was written when I held a research post funded by the German Federal Ministry of Education and Research.

Image 1

Diagram of hexagrams sent by Joachim Bouvet from Pékin to Gottfried Wilhelm Leibniz in 1700; received in Berlin in 1701. Arabic numerals added by Leibniz. 87,74 x 74,01 cm.

LK-MOW Bouvet 10, Bl. 27-28. Leibniz-Archiv. Niedersächsische Landesbibliothek, Hannover.

Image 2

龔賢、山水圖
Gong Xian, *Landscape and Trees*, c. 1679.
Album leaf. Ink on paper. 15.9 x 19.1 cm.

The Metropolitan Museum of Art, New York / bpk. From the P. Y. and Kinmay W. Tang Family Collection. Gift of Wen and Constance Fong in honour of Mr. and Mrs. Douglas Dillon, 1979.

Image 3

Paul Cézanne, *Mont Sainte-Victoire*, c. 1902-6. Oil on canvas. 57.2 x 97.2 cm.

The Metropolitan Museum of Art, New York. The Walter H. and Leonore Annenberg Collection. Gift of Walter H. and Leonore Annenberg, 1994. Bequest of Walter H. Annenberg, 2002.